SONGS OF THE ETONIC

SONGS OF THE ETONIC

D.K. SPENCER

Songs of the Etonic

Library of Congress Control Number: 2021919507

ISBN 978-1-7376005-1-0

The sea shanties, *Cape Cod Girls* and *Anchors Aweigh,* are in the public domain, written in mid eighteen-hundred and early nineteen-hundred, and are printed under fair use. U.S. Copyright applies to material written after 1923.

The Ol' Gen-Ones and *Load'n Ore for the Company Man* are original songs by the author.

Cover Art by Joe Bergeron - Fellow, International Association of Astronomical Artists

Printed in the United States.

For Gary

Who taught me that to stalemate
Is always better than to win.

PREFACE

Songs of the Etonic portrays the optimism of space travel of the 1950's and 60's. While molten uranium and blast furnace propulsion are meant as levity, a dark underlying seriousness remains.

Conceived in 1957, and later developed by General Atomic, the starship Orion was to propel itself three-hundred-forty-thousand mph, utilizing 2,782 one-kilo-pulse-units, aka atomic bombs. Each three hundred pound bomb would be ejected at .86 second intervals. By riding continuous atomic shock waves, Orion would be able fly to Mars by 1963, and on to Saturn by 1970.[1]

Beyond the absurdity of using nuclear bombs to propel a starship, the lack of proficient shielding of the crew from radiation was a major concern, as touched on in my story.

The atomic starship Orion was funded for more than a decade, and aspects of the design are still in use today.

1. Statistics from, Project Orion, by George Dyson, published by Henry Holt and Company, LLC. 115 West 18th Street, New York, New York 10011.

Sexism was alive and well in the 1950's and 60's and therefore the characters in this story are all men. Least we forget, the fields of aerodynamics, astrophysics, and engineering were almost, if not entirely, dominated by men. The story does, however, point out this absurdity by highlighting how the particularly lopsided dynamic brings out the worst in the crew, who fight and drink without the presence of women to help temper them. These are all themes consistent with the era.

The Flubber element within this story comes from the 1961 film, "The Absent Minded Professor" which was based on the short story "A Situation of Gravity" by Samuel W. Taylor, written in 1943. Later marketed by Hasbro in 1962 as a child's toy, Flubber is composed of borax and polyvinyl alcohol.

Borax is a chemical compound containing Boron which is used to slow nuclear fission. It should be noted that Flubber's neutron-capturing properties to shield from radiation or otherwise control nuclear fission are purely theoretical. One ought not try this at home.

SONGS OF THE ETONIC

Walking toward his new commission, Cal spies what is to be his new home away from Earth, for the foreseeable future. Parked with silvery fin-points resting on the pad, the Etonic is readying for launch. Older and crustier than Cal had envisioned, it looks like a rusty barge heading down the Willamette. And the crew even older and crustier! How will he make it, he wonders? Unsure this mission was the right decision, his stomach begins to knot.

Looking mostly like a series of rusty old pipes and barrels piled together with a nose cone on top, the Etonic was not crafted with aesthetics in mind, but instead designed by committee out of practicality and budgetary constraints. Every inch looks to Cal as though it's been through the depths of hell and back. There are more than a few odd-sized repair plates bolted in various places, and scorch marks are visible around all sides of the hull. The ship sure has seen some history he thinks, wondering how the rocket can fly at all?

Boarding the ship, he notices the crew has split into two sections. The flight crew of six are heading up the elevator to the upper levels nearer the nose cone, while a dozen or more crewmen crowd into the lower compartments that hold engineering, and the engine room proper.

Joining the flight crew Cal heads to the elevator. Coming out of the Academy with a specialty in engine physics and space flight navigation ensures a seat up top, he reasons. But his luck doesn't turn that way.

"I'm sorry sir, can I see your orders?" the steward asks.

"Sure," says Cal, handing him the tablet.

"Yes, I was right, you're down in the engineering section ahead of the ore room."

"I was afraid of that. By the way, what's the *ore room?*"

The steward eyes Cal funny, "The ore room is where they put the ore." He pauses, sizing-up the young space Engineer. "You're familiar with a Gen-One, sir?"

"Yes, of course," Cal lies.

So, that's what we're carrying. I'm not too far off, I am on an old rusty barge.

"Good luck, sir."

"Thank you," says Cal, not catching the steward's jest.

Shuffling behind what are to become his crewmates, and though he's at least thirty years younger than the next youngest man, Cal does his level best to blend in. Throwing his duffle over shoulder, Cal places his hands on the smooth metal railings, as he climbs the ladder into the bowels of the ship. As soon as he enters, he's hit with the unmistakable odor of stale body sweat.

"I guess Doc wasn't lying about that," Cal says to no one in particular.

He notices the jar-like fixtures illuminating the dimly lit passageway. If Cal squints and tilts his head, the ship's interior looks and feels more like a submarine than a starship. He wonders if he'll fit in here? He doesn't see how.

Being young and inexperienced is not an advantage. Surrounded by unfamiliar and antiquated tech doesn't help either. All the usual fears are cropping up.

Coming to the bulkhead of his assigned room Cal is relieved to have his own quarters, he's looking forward to putting his feet up and resting. Opening the metal hatch looking in, Cal sees thirteen Black, Anglo, and Latino faces quizzically peering back at him. Apparently, he will *not* be having a cabin to himself after all.

Cal flashes on an image of his father working in the mines, he's surprised to see similar faces. He hadn't expected the Gen-Ones to be crewed by these old men, men attempting to escape poverty.

According to his history-vids, in the early stages, space travel was a risky but lucrative venture. The element of risk created the demand for engine room specialists. Because of the risk, the job pays well.

Job security and a solid paycheck are all the allure these men needed. Working and dying on a Gen-One is a far better prospect than not working at all, Cal reasons.

Beyond the faces, Cal notices bunk after bunk lining the walls. The room is dark and cramped, and the men sit with legs dangling over making small talk to one another. Spying the only empty bunk up top, Cal and duffel pile-in.

Perfect, just perfect.

"Hi," says a scrawny but muscular Anglo man with weathered features. He's dressed in the company uniform, blue pinstripes on a gray flannel jumpsuit like the others. He could be fifty or seventy, it's tough to tell.

"Let me introduce you to the boys. We're going to be spending a lot of time together, and not in the best of conditions, so we might as well get to know each other lickity-split. I'm Rex."

"I'm Cal. I just graduated from the Academy with a degree in Engineering, with emphasis on particle physics."

"Well Cal," says Rex, ignoring Cal's presumptuous qualifications, "this is Dixon, and Mallory over there. Daniel to your right, that's Elroy, and next to him is Chip and Jimmy. Ernie is up on your left, and Rodriguez is next to him, then Joey.

"Walter is in the bunk below you. Be careful of Walter when you go up and down. He doesn't like being jostled. That leaves Tennessee, Merle, Travis, and Nathan over there, in that cubby of bunks—next to the laundry tub. By the way, everyone does their own laundry here.

"Don't worry about trying to remember names right now, Kid. The one you do have to remember is Rusty. Rusty is our most experienced crewman. If you have a question about anything...anything son, Rusty can help you out. We're a team, Kid. Understood? We help each other, it's the only way.

"That there, standing in the bulkhead is Rusty. Rusty is Engineer First Class. As an officer his quarters are across the way. But you'll see him most days in engineering, pitchin' ore like the rest of us."

Rusty's ruddy and knurled face looks like it met its match with a can opener. It suits him somehow. Well past 60, skinny but muscular for a man his age, Rusty looks as healthy and fit as a man in his mid-forties. It's clear that Rusty is the alpha dog by the way he commands the room, even when he's not in it.

Stepping off his bunk Cal gives Rusty an Academy solute. "Sir. I'll do my part, sir."

"Hmmp," says Rusty. "They keep sending me these greenhorns to train. No offense kid, just do your best to stay out of the way. This isn't the Academy and we do serious work here. Stay out of the way, pay attention, and ask questions...Better yet, just stay out of the way."

"Aw Kid," says Rex. "Don't worry, he don't mean it. You'll warm up to him."

"It's fine," says Cal. "Close quarters here, so we'll make it work."

"That's what I like to hear Kid."

Though Cal has met everyone, it doesn't feel like it. He's heard a bunch of names he can't match with faces to save his life.

Ten minutes in and I already have a nickname, 'Kid,' Cal chuckles to himself. *And it feels like it's going to stick. Could be worse I guess.*

Cal makes himself at home, unfurling a bedroll atop his bunk. Stepping back down over some legs, Cal heads through the hatch and into the passageway. He wants to explore the ship before it blasts-off in an hour. Though he has to admit crewing on an ore barge won't be the most exciting of missions. If he can familiarize himself with the ship, he'll be better prepared to perform his duties. He's nervous about this old technology, itchy for the solid footing of his Academy training on newer equipment. And these old men. The Academy hosts all sexes. He'll miss seeing a diversity of gender on this long voyage.

The Etonic is beyond old. Cal didn't realize these old rockets were still flying. He'd learned about Gen-Ones in his history-vids.

History-vids! We are so beyond these old contraptions. I don't even want to know how to keep this barge afloat and navigating in the right direction.

History-vids or no, Cal isn't prepared for what he finds in the next room.

Popping over the bulkhead into engineering, Cal's eyes widen, taking in the brightly colored panels of flashing lights and dials, oscilloscopes, valves, meters, rheostats, oscillators, and oddly enough what looks like a Theremin, and a Jacobs ladder. To Cal's eye, all completely useless engineering antiquity of questionable value for space flight.

"They can't possibly fly this way," Cal says to no one in particular, the knot in his stomach tightening. "I feel sick. Is it too late to get off, I wonder?"

"Everyone feels that way the first time," says Mallory.

"Oh, I didn't see you in here. Sorry, I just wasn't expecting such...such..."

"Such a heap pile of junk?" Mallory offers.

"I wasn't going to say that, I was going to say...Aw, you're right. It is a heap pile of junk!"

"It's okay. Working the controls comes second nature soon enough."

"Now I am scared."

Mallory laughs. "Well, at least you're honest. It's not that bad. We've all learned how to use this old equipment. We'd be lost on a new ship."

"I mean how can you even use a Theremin to fly a ship? Or a Jacobs ladder for that matter? Tell me how this stuff is useful?"

"We fiddle with 'em to relieve the monotony. Some nights Merle or maybe Tennessee will start us off singing. Sometimes it's Travis. The Theremin comes in real handy.

"Ah, can I show you around engineering?"

Bewildered, Cal follows Mallory down the passageway toward the engine room and the main thruster rockets. The temperature becomes noticeably warmer. Passing into a rather large room, Cal notices a small cart and rail system loaded with ore.

"This must be what we're ferrying for export."

"This is the ore room," says Mallory waving his arms.

"Can't be all there is? The payload has to bigger than just this room, doesn't it? There must be a larger section near the nose? Or further aft?"

"No, this is the ore room, not payload containment," Mallory laughs. "That's mid-ship. We're hauling magnetite for a new technology, not exactly sure—it's kind of hush-hush."

"I still don't understand. We're not hauling ore to some planet that needs ore?"

"No, this ore is for propulsion, Kid. You think it's our cargo? Ah, ha-hah." Mallory's lingering grin turns to a hearty laugh.

"That's a new one Kid. Wait'll the guys hear this one."

Stepping over the bulkhead, Mallory mutters down

the passageway. "Wait till they hear. Thinks we're hauling ore. Ah, ha-ha."

Grimacing, Cal hears him echoing all the way down.

Still not making sense, Cal looks at the carts and then at the piles of ore. Following the rails into the engine room he sees what looks like a furnace box. From there a conveyor leads into a sealed anti-room, the core chamber visible through tempered and tinted glass just beyond. Then it hits him.

Oh, my God! They're burning raw uranium! We moved past blast-furnace propulsion half a century ago. Molten ore runs into the Thermatron creating a chain reaction that incites a plasma field. It's like boiling water with fission. Sure, it works, but it is so inefficient, not to mention dangerous.

And the radiation from the ore? How are the men protected? These old engines can't still be in service?

Interrupting Cal's train of thought, Rusty enters the ore room.

"What's this I hear about cargo," trying to stifle a laugh, but can't quite. "That's the funniest thing I've ever heard, Kid. They teach you that at the Academy, do they?"

"No sir." A bead of sweat runs down his brow.

"Well son, I got to stoke some ore into the box. We're getting ready to blast-off. You can go back and strap down or you can stay and load ore. I can teach you a few ropes that you can't learn lying down."

"Thank you sir, I'll stay. I need to learn. I welcome the chance," he says, though the thought of being exposed to uranium for months and months makes him angry. His dad died from over exposure. Cal thinks about mentioning this, then thinks better of it. He needs to fit in. If the old men are good with it, then he'll have to be.

"Well good, son, I'm pleased with your attitude. We get some kids so green they can't get out of the bunk room. Glad you're not one of 'em.

"Hand me that pickaxe over there. The larger chunks have to be broken down. Grab that shovel, start loading ore from the cart, pitch it into the furnace box. You got that?"

"I think I can handle it, sir. Here's your pick," says Cal, turning the memory of his dad over in his mind.

Reluctantly, Cal begins shoveling ore. Who'd have thought? His dad shoveled uraninite in the mines every day, and look what it got him? Still, he would have been proud, though Cal knows what he would've said.

Why'd you go to the Academy to pitch ore? I can teach you that in about ten seconds. Makes no sense, Son...

Rusty and Cal work together for half an hour. Cal has a pretty good fire stoked in the box. Rusty gives an approving glance, nodding toward the bunk room.

"Come on Kid, we gotta strap down, blast-off in aught-thirty," says Rusty walking back to his quarters.

Entering the bunk room, Cal jumps-up inadvertently placing his foot on Walter's shoulder, sliding into his bunk.

"Hey, watch it!" complains Walter.

"Sorry," returns Cal. He's suddenly nervous thinking about the liftoff. He's been through various simulations at the Academy, but none have prepared him for blasting off in the Etonic.

Strapped into his bunk, Cal is surprised by his own anticipation. He's heard how exciting it is.

The waiting is worse than the g-forces!

After what seems like forever, he hears the final countdown. Feeling a great low rumble, at first far off then much closer, Cal readies himself checking his blast-straps one last time.

Many of the men hold small crosses on chains around their necks. The entire ship begins to shake and shimmy. It woggles, shudders, and jerks, feeling to Cal like the whole ship is coming apart. This motion lasts for an inordinate amount of time, long enough for Cal to think something might be wrong. Were they going to explode? The shaking gives way to a sudden lurch and an unending roar. The men let go of their crosses to grasp their ears. Cal follows suit, plugging his ears with his fingers.

The more experienced men smile at each other. They've been through this at least fifteen times or more.

Cal acknowledges Mallory in the top bunk next to him. "Is this shaking normal?"

"Yeah, don't worry. The ship is building up momentum for the long galactic voyage.

"We just passed the Kármán Line."

After a long twenty minutes the roaring stops. All personal effects not bolted down begin to float for a few minutes until ship gravitation is suddenly reactivated, causing Cal's duffle to hit him in the head.

"That's it!" says Rusty. "The burn is over, but the box is empty."

Understanding the meaning, the crew unbuckles, readying themselves for their assigned shifts. The men's duties will rotate from shift to shift for the next twenty-seven months. Their routine is simple, or so Cal has been instructed.

Four men set out for the galley to prepare three days of meals for the men in engineering, and the flight crew up top. Seven of the men, including Cal stay put in their bunks. It's their shift to rest. Their work will begin in a day or two.

Creating a redundancy in skills ensures the safety of ship and crew. The remaining men head for the engine room where they will load ore for the next three days. Crewmen trade their pre-assigned duties with the precision of a ballet.

After a couple of weeks, Cal begins to feel the rhythm of rotating shifts.

Beginning to understand the peculiarities of the ship, Cal heads to the ore room where Joey and Dixon are speaking in low, hushed tones. When Cal enters, they suddenly stop.

Joey, a wiry old man standing about five-foot-four says, "Hey Kid, we got a job for you."

"Yeah," says Dixon. "We have to clean the tubes and check the linings. You'll have to go down the gangway past the reactor core. There, you'll open the hatch to access the tube linings. Here, put this rad-suit on. I'll run you through the steps."

"Sure thing, Dixon," responds Cal, totally unsure of himself.

Pulling on the orange radiation suit over his gray jumpsuit, Cal affixes a blue respirator over the top of his forehead in compliance with Dixon's wishes.

"Good," says Dixon. "Now you need to roll up your pant legs so you don't track tube lint back past the access panel. You don't want to contaminate the ship, okay?"

"Okay, but won't I need the suit for protection? How do I protect my legs from radiation?"

"They don't teach you that at the Academy? Well, there's negative static pressure down at knee level, so the radiation never settles along the catwalk. You'll be fine."

Sounding like bullshit, Cal proceeds to roll up his pant legs anyway. The whole process feels counterintuitive.

"That's good, Kid, now your sleeves. Roll up your sleeves to your elbows and put these blue chem-gloves on. The gloves offer far more protection and they won't fit around the bulk of your clothing anyhow. So, roll 'em up."

Uncomfortable, Cal complies with Dixon's directions. He hasn't been trained to clean tube linings, so he's forced to trust his fellow crewmen.

"Great, Kid, now one last thing. Take this whiskbroom to dust off the lining. If you see something out of place or damaged, report back with the location and tile number. Got it?

"Here, you'll need this."

Dixon hands Cal a flashlight and a scratch pad.

"There you go, Kid. Good luck."

Cal proceeds nervously down the gangway past the Thermatron core, towards the bulkhead access panel.

"Wait, Kid!" Says Dixon walking down the gangway, "I almost forgot. Put this kerchief over your head and tie it under your chin. This keeps any radioactive dust particles from settling into your hair.

"Good, Kid. That looks good."

"Are you sure this is right?" Cal asks, looking just like a babushka.

"Sure," says Dixon. "Perfect."

Unbeknownst to Cal, Dixon has been the distraction affording Joey time to suit up and slip unnoticed into the Thermatron chamber. He's holding something in his gloved hands.

Feeling like a clown, Cal proceeds past the bulkhead down the gangway toward the core. Encountering the locked access panel, he struggles with the hatch release. He hasn't been given the code.

"It appears to be locked," Cal calls-out, just as Joey slips back out of the core, unnoticed.

"Yeah, it sticks sometimes. Try turning around and put your back into it," Dixon yells.

"It's hard to get any leverage, just a minute."

Turning around Cal finds half the crew in the passageway struggling to get a better look at the fool with a broom, a flashlight, and a blue handkerchief on his head. Pointing, they all begin to laugh hysterically, while Joey blends back in with the crowd to guffaw and chortle with the others.

"Very funny guys," says Cal, walking back up the gangway just as Rusty steps over the bulkhead.

"What the devil's going on here? What're y'all doin'?"

The men attempt to flee, but Rusty is standing between them and the exit.

"Someone please tell me what's going on? Why are you all crammed into the gangway? What the devil...? Who is that?"

Unable to help himself, Rusty begins to laugh with the other crewmen. The broom, the rolled-up pant legs, the handkerchief? A flashlight?

Regaining himself, Rusty says, "Kid, come out of there.

We're going to get to the bottom of this. All of you go into engineering. None of you are leaving until I clear this up."

"It's my fault, Rusty," says Dixon. "We had to have an initiation for the Kid and the time was ripe."

"Ripe may be, but y'all know better than to create a situation that can go horribly wrong. Now I know there's probably little danger to the ship, but Cal hasn't been trained for work on this old bucket of andirons. He might have inadvertently hurt himself or endangered the crew.

"Dixon, since you claim responsibility, you're going to get off a little easier than if you hadn't. You're peeling potatoes for the next two weeks. That's after you've completed your other shifts. For the rest of you..."

Rusty pauses thinking better of it, "You all get back to work. I won't write you up this time, but if it happens again... Rusty shakes his head, then looks to Cal.

"Cal, come on, son, I want to have a word with you."

Reluctantly, a fully humiliated Cal walks over to Rusty. "Yes, sir?"

"Kid, they're testing you to be sure, but they're also just blowing off a little steam. I'll keep an eye out, but I think they'll leave you alone for a while. What're you thinking, son? That has to be one of the funniest pranks they've pulled-off yet."

"I don't know, sir. I wasn't expecting it, sir. They told me to dust off the tube linings, report any tiles that might need replacing. I wanted to do my part. I guess I was just too eager and didn't think things through."

"Tube linings!!? Ha, Kid there's no such thing as tube linings on this ship or any of the Gen-Ones. I guess you didn't know that. Don't be too hard on yourself, we all go through something like this trying to fit in. The boys aren't sure whether to accept you yet and they're just trying to test your mettle. Hold your ground, things will work themselves out.

"Now get back to work. And pull that silly kerchief off your head."

Two hours later the whole crew, except Rusty, heads to the mess for an evening meal. Rusty rarely eats with the rest of the crew, preferring to eat alone in his quarters. He is served in his room just out of earshot of the galley.

As they form a line to the mess, Cal brings up the tail end. Still smarting from the embarrassment earlier, he tries to ignore the inevitable jokes and jabs that will be coming his way. He knows he somehow needs to prove himself, but he just can't figure out how. If he doesn't, he'll always be the new kid.

One by one, the men file past the cook as he plops some gray-looking mass on their plates. They sit in various places at a long metal table, picnic style. Though from outward appearances the men don't look like the picnicking type.

Cal tries to edge in between Dixon and Joey, but the space is too small. He asks Joey politely if he wouldn't mind scooting over a little.

"Why don't you ask Dixon, Kid? He can make room just as easily as I can."

"I can ask Dixon, but I'm asking you politely. I need a little more room, that's all."

Joey is not having it. He won't move for a 'tube cleaner'.

That got some laughs.

"Look Joey, I just want to sit so I can eat my meal like everyone else."

"Well, you ain't like everyone else, now are you? I ain't moving so what are you gonna do about it, tube boy?"

Joey gets up off the bench, as the rest of the crew quietly watches the drama play out. This is great entertainment for such a long voyage.

"I don't want trouble Joey, but if there's no avoiding it, then I'll stand up for myself. What's it going to be, Joey?"

"Look the Kid's got spunk, who would'a guessed?"

Slightly smaller in build, but strong from pitching ore, Joey grabs Cal by the neck. Wrapping round his arm, he begins socking Cal with his fist. Cal struggles, but manages to pop Joey in the eye, exacerbating the mood of the crowd. The shipmates begin yelling and screaming, taking bets on who is going to win the round. Sensing Joey's dilemma, Dixon stands up to hold Cal's arms, allowing Joey to unabatedly jab Cal in the stomach.

Having witnessed the hazing earlier in the day and now watching this squabble unfold, Rodriguez has had enough. He's had his share from these boys in years past. This fight a salty reminder. Sinewy, but stronger and taller, he begins to roundhouse, pounding Joey in the ribs, and knocking him in the jaw with a jab.

He turns back to Dixon who falls with one punch to the forehead. It's a beautiful sight for those on the sidelines, but as the brawl gets going, the whole crew enters the fracas.

Fists are flying and so is the blood, as noses are knocked out of joint and eyes are blackened. Cuts and bruises are handed out for the asking.

The fight is a symphony of pummeling fists and shaky legs, and Rusty walks in right at the crescendo.

"What the hell is happening? Who's responsible here?" shouts Rusty. "Well, let's have it. Who started this and why do you boys always do this every other Friday? Goddamn, you're like clockwork."

Joey pipes up, "It's the Kid fault, Rusty. He tried to shoe-horn in between me and Dixon, all rude like, then before I knows it, he jacks me one."

Cal begins to protest, but Rodriguez sets the record straight.

"No, sir, it didn't happen like that. In fact, Joey started the whole thing and Dixon poured on the gasoline. I tried to settle the score to calm the place down but I guess maybe we all got a little carried away."

"Carried away. Yeah, I'd like someone to carry you all away. How old are you men? You all still bite and scratch like a bunch of teenagers. Look, I know you boys got to blow off steam, but not every frickin' week.

"Look, you all should be punished and I'll write this up in the book, you can be sure of it...but you all know I can't spare a one a you, so you have me over a barrel. If you break out in another fight, I'll be forced to take the worst offenders to the brig and you know what that means. Mandatory probation, a demotion, and a pay cut.

"So, what am I to do with you? I'm going to do something I know I shouldn't. I shouldn't do it. It's unorthodox and you don't deserve it. But it's been a while since you've had a chance to relax. You got to promise me you all have your hostilities out. No more tonight. I'm serious. In exchange, I'll break out two cases of beer."

"Yeaaah!" The men cheer in unison, as the mood lightens instantaneously. The men crowd around Rusty like a school of frenzied fish.

"Wait a minute, let me finish! In exchange, I want you to stop your fighting. That's it. There's no reason for it."

Rusty shakes his head as he unlocks the beer fridge. He knows alcohol can make things worse and his gesture can be seen as reward for bad behavior. But from past experience, he also knows if the boys aren't allowed to blow off steam, it *will* be worse. It's better to get a handle on it now, he figures. The lesser of evils.

Passing beers around, Rusty joins the men, as they all settle down drinking to their hearts content. Loosening up, the men take to Cal, recounting how he socked Joey in the eye and how Rodriguez gave Dixon a couple a punches to remember him by.

Sensing the timing is right, Tennessee hums the pitch of a familiar melody, while Merle waves his hand like a spastic conductor perturbing the electron field. The Theremin wails otherworldly.

whorroo-oooha errrahhoooah, whorroo-oooha...

With Tennessee's voice and electrons in alignment, he nods to Travis. *It's time.* Adjusting the spark frequency to four-four time, Travis twists the rheostat on the Jacobs ladder, watching the spark grow wider as it crawls up the two antennae. A purple flame crescendos then disappears, sparking the light fantastic.

Zap—Zap—Zap—Zap | Zap—Zap—Zap—Zap

Blending their instruments, the ensemble looks and sounds like it's coming from inside Frankenstein's lab.

The juxtaposition of weirdly, spacey sounds and the crackle of Jacobs ladder settle the men down into a quiet, meditative state. This works every time and no one knows why?

whorro-ooha—Zap-Crackle—errrahhoooah—Zap-

Satisfied with the pitch and the beat, Tennessee, Travis, and Merle, famous for raising the men's spirits, set the whole crew off in boisterous song. The men sing...*Cape Cod Girls.*

> *Cape Cod girls ain't got no combs... Haul away, haul away... They brush their hair with codfish bones... Bound, bound away for Alpha Centauri!...*

Mallory nods to Cal, raising his beer. Rex and Walter shout the words because neither can carry a tune.

> *Cape Cod kids ain't got no sleds... Haul away, haul away... They slide down the hills on codfish heads... And we're bound away for Alpha Centauri!*

whorrroo-oooha—Zap-Crackle—errrahhoooah...

"Hey!" They all yell in the spontaneity of the moment. Chip, Jimmy, and Daniel, swing their bottles, singing...

*Cape Cod girls ain't got no frills... Haul away, haul
away... They tie their hair with codfish gills...
Bound, bound away for Alpha Centauri!*

Elroy takes a swig from his bottle, joining Rodriguez and
Nathan to joyfully project...

*Cape Cod cats ain't got no tails... Haul away, haul
away... They lost them all in the northeast gales...
And we're bound away for Alpha Centauri!*

As the men sing, Joey and Dixon sit solemnly in the
corner greedily drinking their beer. In spite of their
present circumstances, they're smugly satisfied knowing
that a larger plan is afoot.

The rest of the crew is ready to sing the night into
morning. Nothing moves the men like tradition, and
Tennessee has just the song to keep them singing.
Humming a few bars, he cues the men.

"And a one, and a two, ..."

whorroo-oooha, begins Merle.

Zap—Zap, plays Travis.

They all know the tune. Cal's heard his father sing this
song many times. It's an old miner's song. With Ernie and
Elroy on tenor, Walter, and Paxton on bass, they belt out
each word with gusto, sing-shouting...

LOAD'N ORE FOR THE COMPANY MAN

Some say-what-a-man is worth... What a-man-is-worth, is a day in the dirt... Dirt and grime, dirt and grime... A man's worth ain't nothing but a dime.

Load'n ore all day... and ore all night... One day sicker and one day done... Lord, don't ya bother me, I've got no plan... Just load'n ore for the company man...

Work'n at night with the moon up ahead... Use my shovel to face my dread... Born to pitch, born to pitch... Pitch'n ore, with no time to bitch.

I was born on a hot summer day... Drink'n and fight'n my only way... Stand the heat, to load the core... Breaking my back, can't stop my chore... Can't go back to my life before.

If I'm mad, you'd better run!... One fist, two is sure to stun... One thing sure, you'll see some action... I'm an un-control-able chain reaction.

GESTURING WITH THEIR HANDS, Rex and Rusty harmonize the final chorus. The whole crew joins in...

Load'n ore all day... and ore all night... One day sicker and one day done... Lord, don't ya bother me, I've got no plan... Just load'n ore for the company man...

The men drink, sing and play through the night until the beer is gone and the Theremin's busted. Playing with the Jacobs ladder, Walter nearly electrocutes Elroy. Those that can crawl, head for their bunks. Others sprawl onto the floor or slump over the mess table. The morning shift comes early, the unlucky bearing the worst of it.

"My head is pounding," says Elroy.

"Mine too," says Jimmy.

"You're all a bunch of school girls," says Paxton.

"Says who?" asks Elroy.

"Knock it off all of you, you heard what Rusty said. Now get to pitching ore," says Mallory. It goes on like this for the rest of their shift.

WEEKS LATER, the ship is running efficiently like the intricate workings of an atomic clock. Engineering has had very little contact with the flight crew, which is an added relief. Less static from the officers the better, they all agree.

In rotation, Cal joins Rodriguez and Elroy in the galley, where they'll be cooking meals for the next three days. As Cal and Rodriguez converse, Elroy listens intently from the sidelines. It's the most fun he's had considering the dull routine of his chores. Usually, he's stuck with Paxton cleaning toilets, or greasing ore cart bearings.

"So Cal, it looks like Joey and Dixon have been giving you wide berth," says Rodriguez.

"Yeah, there's something a little off about those two. Can't quite put my finger on it. They aren't very friendly. Fortunately, I haven't had a shift with them for a while."

"That's good. You seem to be fitting in just fine."

"Good enough," says Cal, filling a steel pot with filtered water. The three are preparing a soup broth, and synth-ham sandwiches for the crew's lunch.

"Say Rodriguez, do you know where we're headed? Strikes me as odd that we're not briefed about our mission. Doesn't that bother you?"

"No, they never tell us. I don't guess the officers figure we matter," says Rodriguez, chopping carrots. "You kinda get used to it.

"They do all the navigation up top. We're probably headed to Canis Major, to the planet Acanthus. It orbits a small sun just off Aludra. That's where we've gone the last several missions."

Cal puts the large pot on boil and greases a fry pan.

"What's special about Acanthus?"

"I don't know, we're confined to the outposts, we're not allowed off-base. Most guys spend their time gambling and cavorting. Plenty of expats live on Acanthus, so there's always something interesting to do."

"I didn't figure you for a gambler, Rodriguez?"

"Oh, I'm not. I prefer to spend my time stargazing the neighboring galaxies in the night sky. I can't get enough of it. That's the one thing about this starship I wish were different. If it were up to me, I'd a put a window or two in this rock-bucket. The view here gets pretty stale."

"Among other things," says Cal, washing his hands, drying them on his apron.

"Windows would be nice, and additional shielding in the ore room for starters."

"Yeah, I guess as long as you're dreaming," says Elroy, slicing a loaf of bread for sandwiches.

"What do you find so interesting about nebulae?" Cal asks, searing a pile of synth-ham on the hot skillet. Elroy steals a piece.

"Have you ever seen the Cartwheel Galaxy? It's a beautiful phenomenon. It looks just like a perpetually exploding firework. Magenta wisps of stellar dust and gases? Stars and planets are slowly, profoundly being drawn into a red dwarf. Someday, long from now, it all gets pulled into a black hole."

"Sounds incredible," says Cal. He's only seen three-dimensional star charts at the Academy, and those are simulations.

"Where does the hole go?" asks Elroy. "Is the universe slowly loosing air?"

"Not air, but gases, stars, and planets. Think of it like a bathtub drain," says Rodriguez.

"What if the drain gets clogged?" asks Elroy. "Does the universe back-up?"

"Never mind," says Rodriguez, seasoning the broth.

"That's enough out of you Elroy," says Cal.

Rodriguez wipes his hands on his apron and pulls a box of instant custard out from the cabinet.

"There's another system I call the Wild-Eyed Beast. Two spiral galaxies colliding together. One is stripping the stars and planets away from the other. Galaxies Xsose and Anthros. We'll get a crazy view from Acanthus."

"That does sound crazy. You have a thing for dying star systems?" asks Cal.

"I hadn't thought about it like that until now. I guess you're right."

Cal turns the skillet down to simmer.

"One of the reasons I got into this line of work is for the adventure. I like it all, the stars, the planets, the galaxies, the inhabitants...But I'm still bothered that the crew is not privy to the mission. And where are the crew women?"

"No really, it's always like this. And as for crew women, it's thought that running a Thermatron is too dangerous," says Rodriguez, frothing the dessert custard.

"That's not the way it works on the new starships. Engineering tech, Navigation, the Helm, are all on the Bridge. And there are equal numbers of women as men."

"I hear tell stories," says Elroy, helping to cut hardened gel protein that's going into what they call 'lunch meat'.

"Times are changing," says Rodriguez. "I hear there're even a few female captains!"

"No," says Elroy. "Can't be."

"Rodriguez is right. Women have turned out to be invaluable in the space program. They make even better pilots for some reason. It's a wonder we've gotten as far as we have without them," says Cal setting out the mess.

"High time, if you ask me," says Rodriguez. "Maybe then the men would shower more often."

"That would be a nice change," says Elroy. "But I don't see how a breeder reactor can be contained on the Bridge?"

Cal laughs. "No, we've come a long way from needing plasma and breeder reactors. I guess you don't realize, but you're on a working antique. You're inside a technological museum! This wonderful piece of machinery is being phased out. Being replaced with the latest and greatest.

"That being a dialectic-particle engine."

"A what'cha whose it?" asks Elroy.

"Never mind," says Rodriguez. "You'll never see one. We're too old. They'll never train us for the job, that's up to you, Cal."

"Your not too old, neither of you," says Cal, but he knows Rodriguez is right.

"You're young, Cal. You'll see a lot of changes in your lifetime. I envy you."

"Well, I'm sure learning a lot on the Etonic, though I must admit it's nothing I've trained for. I just make it up along the way."

"That's why you fit in, Cal," says Rodriguez. "That's all any of us do. One foot in front of the other."

"So, Rodriguez, you know anything about us carrying a payload of magnetite?"

"Yes, but that's just a rumor. Our cargo is kept secret. It's above our pay-grade. But the rumor's out there."

"It's interesting that the crew cannot be trusted with either the destination of the ship, nor the hold of its cargo.

"If it is magnetite, I can see why it's secret. Magnetite might be the latest answer for inter-dimensional travel. It might also be used as a super-bomb. So yeah, if that's the cargo we're carrying..."

"Right," says Rodriguez, "and should we collide with anything or should anything collide with us, the shock-wave will travel at a force for a half a light year. You better keep that under your hat though, Cal.

"You, too, Elroy. No sense in worrying the crew 'cause we don't know if it's true.

"Even if we are carrying magnetite our mission doesn't change. And as the uppers always say, we don't..."

Suddenly Cal and Rodriguez are thrown violently into the kitchen counter, and Elroy flies out the galley door.

The ship is jolted in violent shakes, throwing most of the crew onto the floor. Something is majorly wrong with propulsion.

Cal hears a funny whining noise. Crewmen's faces appear ashen. They've never felt the ship shake like this or heard this particular noise before. The whine is followed by a shudder, shaking the whole rocket and everyone on it.

Rusty jumps to assess the problem. "Rodriguez," he shouts, "call up to the Bridge...Ask them if they know what's going on? Keep the Bridge from distracting me. Tell them I'm busy finding out what's wrong on our end...And tell them...Tell them I'll talk to them if and when I find something. Clear?"

"Yes sir!" says Rodriguez jumping to the Com.

Instinctively, the crewmen man their stations awaiting further instructions. The entire crew mobilizes, willing to do their part to maintain the safety of the ship.

Except perhaps for two.

Passing engineering, Rusty jumps into the ore room, stopping short of the core lock. Donning an orange rad-suit and a pair of blackout goggles, he peers through the core port, turning the port-glass from opaque to transparent. He sees a fiery glow in the reactor core that appears to be running unusually hot. Looking past the flame, Rusty observes the ram cylinders starting to distort from the heat. He floods the core cavity with boro-alkaline through a system of valves—a temporary measure.

This should buy some time.

Changing the port-glass back to opaque, Rusty heads toward the Com, "Captain? I've slowed our runaway for a time, but it's only temporary. We have an hour, maybe two. I need to find what's causing these wild fluctuations."

"Good work, Chief. Get on it and let me know if there's anything we can do from the Bridge."

"Will do Captain. Chief out."

Without talking to any of the crew, Rusty heads to the lift. He's discovered something out-of-sorts and wants to discuss it with the Captain in private.

The Chief Engineer enters the Bridge,

"Captain, may I have a word?"

"Sure Chief." He gestures toward the ready room.

The room is decorated with a black leather couch, a white acrylic conference table, and matching orange chairs. Sliding their chairs up to the table, Rusty stares at the avocado wall-to-wall shag.

"Sir, I don't want to rattle the men," he says, looking at the Captain. "I think the core has been sabotaged...I'm sure of it, sir."

"Sabotaged? By whom? Someone on the crew? What leads you to this, Rusty?"

"I can't tell for sure, but it looks like the flow manifold has been messed with. There's no other way to explain it, sir. I need to get down into the core to do a more thorough investigation. Once I see the problem, I might be able to reverse it. As it stands, Captain, if I can't stop the reaction, you know what it means."

The Chief looks gravely at the Captain.

"To make matters worse, we have to consider the likely probability that a saboteur is loose on this ship!"

"Do everything you can, Chief, and keep me informed. These Gen-Ones don't have life pods. We need to know one way or the other. I'm sending the XO with you. He'll keep an eye on the men...Oh, and thanks, Rusty. Glad you're on my ship."

"Sir."

Taking the lift down, Rusty heads back to engineering, with Harris close behind. Walking in, he finds several of the crewmen grouped around Cal analyzing the problem.

"Maybe it's only a flow meter," says Nathan.

"No, I checked that," says Rex, "the meter's right. Not sure what it could be."

"It's nothing obvious," says Cal, "The ship wouldn't shudder like that from a small deviation. Something is interfering with the flow of the core."

"Brilliant deduction Cal," says Rusty, entering the room. "You're coming with me. The rest of you stay put until I get a handle on this."

Seeing the concern on the men's faces, Rusty tells them he knows what the problem is. That he can fix it. Both statements are a lie, but the men's faces visibly relax.

"XO Harris is here to report back," Rusty explains. "Captain wants to be informed of the progress, you all stay behind the bulkhead. Now do it!" he shouts.

"It'll protect you from the radiation wash."

Thinking about the temporary fix, Rusty knows the injected boro-alkaline will begin losing its cooling effects soon. Then the reactor will rapidly heat up again.

"Cal, I want you to stay here in the core anti-room. Put on a rad-suit, gloves, and helmet. I may need you to hand me tools depending upon what I find in there. Under no circumstances are you to come into the chamber. You hear me? You do not enter the core, is that understood?"

"Yes sir! Understood...Good luck Chief. Here awaiting orders, sir."

Fully prepped, Rusty clears the failsafe on the reactor panel, entering a sequence of five numbers. Setting his stopwatch, he knows he only has six minutes in the chamber before irreversible blood-cell damage.

Affixing his helmet to his rad-suit, Rusty turns the dial on his tri-mix cylinder to the flow position. The apparatus allows him to breath freely in the chamber. Without protection, the air temperature alone will kill a man in seconds, and the radiation in milliseconds.

Peering into the hellfire, he can see unspent uranium building up in the interior of the heat exchanger. Uranium slag is clogging the intake tubes. But clogged intakes are the symptom, not the problem.

Rusty steps back into the anti-room.

"Cal, hand me a shovel and have a pickaxe at the ready. If this works, I'm buying whiskey tonight."

Cal hands him a shovel, but says nothing.

Pausing briefly, Rusty looks through the tempered glass into engineering where he sees all but two faces of his wide-eyed crewmen. Each of them knows Rusty is risking his life for them. They have no thought for their own safety.

Jumping into the chamber, Rusty uses his shovel as a pry-bar, and begins chipping away at the uranium slag that's building up on the baffles. Removing the slag helps a little, but is only a temporary fix.

It must be something...There it is.

Someone had placed shunts over the intake valves. Whoever it was knew what they were doing. They must have gotten in and back out of the chamber without being seen, or setting off the radiation alarms. In short, only an experienced crewman.

He could understand it. The pay was good, but it wasn't great. Ship life didn't change much and most men died on the job either from accident or old age. That was the truth of it.

These men don't have lives, or homes, or wives. So, why not take a little money and rig the ship? But, that doesn't make sense. How would they get off the ship before it exploded? Maybe they've already enjoyed their money? Or, are they ideologues willing to die for a cause?

Too many questions.

Pondering the problem in front of him, Rusty observes that the shunts are fused to the valves from excessive heat, they can't be knocked off with a shovel.

What will break the bond?

Like a frozen comet to the head, it hits him. Cold on Hot. Strictly outside standard operating procedures, Rusty sees but one chance of saving the crew, the ship, and the cargo.

Holding his breath, Rusty uncouples the hose from the respirator, reaching around to the cylinder on his side. He changes the mixture of his tri-mix, moving the needle all the way to 100% nitrogen, while pumping up the pressure.

Using the air supply hose like a nozzle, he sprays the pressurized nitrogen on the shunts which causes a wild temperature differential.

If I hold here long enough...they'll explode.

Which they do!

Quickly, Rusty resets the tri-mix, returning the cylinder to a normalized pressure, reconnecting the hose back to his respirator. Out of breath, Rusty sits down on the metal grid, realizing he's wiped out. The exertion and heat have taken a toll. He collapses on the metal grate.

Watching through the port, Cal yells, "He did it! Get him out of there! Come on, help me get him out of there!"

Cal shouts to anyone who will listen.

Joey and Dixon race toward the bulkhead before the rest of the men can react.

Still prone, Rusty tries to think who the saboteur could possibly be? Remembering the crew through the tempered glass, two were missing.

Who were absent?

Then he hits on it. Joey and Dixon. Joey is a bit of a hot-head, he always has been. And Dixon is right beside him. They're a pair! That's how they didn't get caught. And they both work pitching ore together!

Then it hits Rusty again. He's been in the Thermatron chamber for nine minutes. Three minutes too long.

"Help me," Cal yells to the crew.

"It's too late, Cal. He's gone," says Dixon.

"No! It's not too late, help me get him out." Struggling with Dixon, Cal enters the access code, pushing him off.

"You'll flood the anti-room with Radiation. Stand down!" yells Dixon.

"NO!" Yells Call. "Rusty is alive, Now help me get him out of there."

"Take it easy," says Joey. "There's nothing we can do now. He's toast."

"I'm not leaving him in there! We can fight over this later. I'm pulling Rusty out."

Cal knocks Dixon down, shoving Joey aside. He enters the chamber as Joey and Dixon scramble out the anti-chamber hatch, slamming it shut. Radiation alarms blare, as radiation floods the anti-room, blasting the sealed bulkhead.

Lying on the reactor floor unconscious, Cal pulls Rusty by the armpits, through the core chamber, across the core bulkhead and into the anti-room, closing the core hatch behind him.

Operating on instinct and adrenaline, Cal eyes an emergency hose labeled Flubber, mounted to the gray metal bulkhead.

Remembering from his history-vids, Cal knows that in addition to being an extremely bouncy substance with incredible rebounding properties, Flubber is most useful as a neutralizer of ionizing radiation.

Aiming the hose, Cal douses Rusty with a lime-green, gooey mixture compound of polyvinyl alcohol, and sodium tetraborate decahydrate.

Cal's quick thinking and Academy training has paid off. If Rusty has a hope or a prayer, it rests in Flubber's lime-green protective goodness.

Flubber plops into bouncy piles onto Rusty's Flubber-covered body resting on the anti-chamber floor.

Rodriguez alerts the Captain on the Com, who sends the ship's doctor to triage the effects of radiation poisoning,

"Everybody get clear," shouts the doctor. "We need space and room to breathe. Rodriguez! Cal! Help move Rusty to his quarters."

Placing Rusty on his bed, the doctor, Cal, and Rodriguez turn Rusty's room into a sterile ICU, putting fresh sheets on his bed, making room for a crash cart and triage equipment.

"Harris, report to the Captain. Inform him of our situation down here. We need medical support and supplies, stat!" demands the Doctor.

"Yes, sir!" the XO replies, racing to the Com.

Two nurses arrive in time to hear Dr. Murray instruct Cal and Rodriguez to vacate the room.

Out of breath, Cal walks toward the hatch, looking the doctor in the eye.

"Rusty saved our lives. Now you save his."

The Doctor injects stabilizers into Rusty's blood to stave off the poisoning. His entire room will be contaminated, but there's nothing to be done about it presently.

Cal and Rodriguez sit with the other men in the mess, awaiting word from the doctor. It seems like hours have passed, waiting for a positive word. There is little chatter amongst the men, most are fidgety and contemplative.

After an expanse of time, Dr. Murray finally emerges from the ICU to addresses the crew.

"After a couple hours of hurried work, Rusty is in a stabilized condition. I'm giving Rusty a full transfusion of highly oxygenated blood. It will extend hope if not life... The prognosis isn't good. But he's got a fair shot at short-term recovery unless his cellular structure has ruptured. The physics of this is fairly cut and dried. Time will tell."

IN THE MESS, later that night the mood is somber, the talk is sullen and depressed. No one wants to talk about what happened today. The crew's thoughts are with Rusty, what might be, and what could have been.

Everyone except Joey and Dixon.

Sorry their botched plan didn't work, they're more worried Rusty might recover. What might he tell the doctor? Maybe they can still get to him before he talks?

The two walk toward Rusty's room, mulling over plans, thinking of ways to keep from being fingered.

"Maybe you put a pillow over his head, see?" says Dixon. "That way, if he struggles he won't be able to yell.

"Nah," says Joey, "I think just a simple holding his mouth and nose shut will do. So as not to raise suspicion."

"You boys up to something?" interrupts the XO walking up beside the men.

"Ah, no," says Dixon. "We were just going to check in on Rusty. Make sure he's okay."

"See he's doing alright," says Joey, shifting in his shoes.

"No you won't. You two won't be leaving my sight," Harris informs. "Captain's orders."

The doctor emerges from Rusty's room to stand at the bulkhead. The solemn crewmen turn their heads to listen.

"We did all that we could..." He pauses. "Rusty has passed. I'm very sorry."

Cal shouts, "Rusty knew! He knew what he was doing. He gave his life for us! He saved the Etonic!"

"Here! Here! For Rusty! Long live Rusty!" the crew instantaneously returns.

ADDRESSING the crew over the Com, the Captain gives his ship-wide condolences for the loss of an officer, a crew member, a friend—Rusty.

"Many knew the Chief over the years, but none like me. Rusty and I have been on the old Gen-Ones since the beginning, when they were the latest and greatest. The newest technology. We've soared through the galaxy on close to seventeen missions together. He was a loyal crewman and has saved countless lives over the years. And now he's saved every life on this ship. Don't you ever forget that, men.

"From all of us on the Etonic, to Rusty—Godspeed! They don't make 'em like that anymore...Capt'n out."

Silent, no one moves or makes a sound. The men, caught in that awkward in-between space where atoms and worlds collide, ponder the profound. Where reality and the impossible are forced to coexist.

Cal can scarcely believe it.

Wasn't it just yesterday, that Rusty was teaching him to pitch ore?

Rusty is shot from a tube, his body floating into deep space, immediately crushing in the vacuum, freezing instantaneously and fracturing apart. His pieces slowly scattering in the solar winds.

It's a spaceman's burial in every respect. It's how a man expects to die, into the void with the whole crew watching.

Merle walks over to the Com, "Captain, if I may?"

"Yes, of course Merle," the Captain replies.

"With Captain's permission, I'd like to give Rusty a proper send-off."

In a low solemn timbre, Merle begins and the crew joins in, signing an old navy traditional...*Anchors Aweigh*.

Anchors Aweigh, my boys,
Anchors Aweigh.
Farewell to foreign shores,
We sail at break of day-ay-ay-ay.

Through our last night ashore,
Drink to the foam,
Until we meet once more.
Here's wishing you a happy voyage home.

Anchors Aweigh.
Sail on to victory
Sink their bones to Davy Jones, hooray!
Anchors Aweigh, my boys,
Anchors Aweigh.

Cal peers at his crewmates. Most are holding back tears. He's unaware of his own. There's a hole in his heart no amount of Flubber can fill. Thinking of his dad, an awkward silence fills the air.

"One more thing," the Captain interrupts.

"Ensigns second class, Joey Filbert and Dixon Perry, are being detained for a formal hearing. We want these guys to be in good shape when we come into port. Their hell is just beginning...That is all."

After a heartbeat of respectful silence and heartfelt sorrow, the crew spontaneously breaks out in ship-wide harmony, singing the Etonic's galactic voyager song.

THE OL' GEN-ONES!

Where are we headed boys?
We're off to Seven Sisters.
Rumbling, spitfire, and noise,
Heading to Seven Sisters.
Keeping watch on the ship's transistors.

On this ol' Gen-One, the ol' Gen-Ones.
Full of fight and whiskey,
On the ol' Gen-Ones, the ol' Gen-Ones.
Our mission's a might bit risky,
On the ol' Gen-Ones, the ol' Gen-Ones!

Look away me boys, what do you see?
Tis that the belt of Orion?
Sailing out in yonder seas,
Deep space we go a fly'n.
Avoiding asteroids, we're a try'n.

We're passin' the dog star Sirius,
Our faith is in the gyro.
Oh, starlight guides to steer us,
Beyond the galactic spiral.
Spirits are high, high on yonder seas.

On this ol' Gen-One, the ol' Gen-Ones.
Full of fight and whiskey,
On the ol' Gen-Ones, the ol' Gen-Ones.
Our mission's a might bit risky,
Lady destiny takes us all on the Ol'—Gen—Ones!!

HAVING SAFELY LANDED at spaceport Ludlow, Cal puts his twenty-seven months voyage in the rear-view mirror. The crewmen from the Etonic disembark, each going their separate ways. Cal says his so-longs, anxious to put the memory of Rusty and the Etonic behind him.

Booking a room at the Hotel Pacifica, his plans include taking a couple weeks of well-deserved R&R, catching up with his old friend and professor Dr. Richardson, and maybe watching a movie in the halo-sim. He has an appointment scheduled with Doc in the morning, but in the meantime Cal intends to relax, put up his feet, and contemplate his future.

Rodriguez, who is also staying at the Pacifica, bumps into Cal at the reservation desk. He suggests they knock back a couple to recount the voyage.

Cal, appreciating how Rodriguez stood up for him, gladly accepts. They head to the Pusser's House for a whiskey and maybe a bite of something that doesn't resemble hardened gel protein.

Knocking back a whiskey, Rodriguez says, "So, Cal, I never got to tell you before, but that was a brave action when you pulled old Rusty out of the core. Why'd you do it? I mean, he probably was a goner already and you put your own life at risk?"

Cal listens, chasing a spud around the simulated protein disk on his plate with a fork.

"You don't have time to think, Rodriguez. You just do what's in front of you. You don't think about it. It's not bravery at all. I don't feel brave."

"Maybe not, but you know as well as I do you were the one that saved the ship. You and Rusty."

"How so?"

"Because, if you hadn't pulled Rusty out of the core we may never have known about the sabotage. And, if we hadn't found that out, the saboteurs would have attempted to do it again.

"If Rusty hadn't told the Doc about finding the shunts in the Thermatron, fingering Joey and Dixon, we all would have blown to Alpha Centauri. And no one would know how or why."

"Yeah, maybe. Just don't go around telling that story to too many people. I don't want the attention. Okay?"

"Sure thing, Cal, no problem. So, do you know where you're going next?"

"No, not yet. My commission has yet to be decided. My plan is to take a couple of weeks off, just soak up a little nothing. How about you?"

"I hear what you mean. That was some heavy stuff we all went through, you in particular. Yeah, I'll be headed out on the Star Gull in a couple of weeks. She's another Gen-One."

"You just can't get enough punishment can you, Rodriguez?"

"Actually, I was ready to retire, but they came to me with an offer I couldn't turn down, and since I know this stuff forwards and backwards, I figure why not? They're doubling my pay. Giving me hardship pay for my experience on the Etonic. I'm sure you'll get something similar."

"Maybe, I'm not going to think about it at the moment."

"Fact is, Cal, and you didn't hear it from me, the higher-ups are going to make you an offer. I can't give you any details, but they need loyal, trustworthy, proven men."

"I'm not loyal, I just do my job and what I hope is the right thing. That's all."

"That's why they want you, Cal. A radical can be turned. You just do the right thing for the right reasons. Anyway Cal, you can pretty much write your own ticket given your performance. It's up to you."

The two finish their meals and discuss their adventures on the Etonic, but never touch on the subject of espionage or Rusty again. Cal admires Rodriguez almost in the same way he had admired Rusty. Steady, levelheaded, in command. That's Rodriguez. That was Rusty.

Eight-forty-five the next morning, Cal walks to Doc's office. He finds that Dr. Richardson is as anxious to hear Cal's stories as Cal is to tell them.

"Hi, Cal, it's good to see you're in one piece."

"Hey, Doc. It's good to be seen in one piece. Do I have stories to tell you! Crewing the Etonic was far crazier than I could've imagined, but somehow it gets in your blood."

"Yes, I know a bit about that...getting into one's blood," the Doc says, remembering his days as Commander of the Star Gazer, a Gen-One heavy cruiser.

"Shall we grab a little breakfast?" asks Cal.

"Why not, Cal? My treat."

Finding a little breakfast spot on campus, they sit at a

sidewalk café known for their synthesized coffee and protein disk pancakes.

The two talk for most of the morning as Cal describes his every impression of the past two-year's experience. He knows the moment of truth is quickly approaching. An offer will be made and he'll need to make a decision that will likely determine the path for the rest of his life.

Should he take the commission if they offer?

Looking back, he's glad he missioned on the Etonic, but would he want to do it all over again? Questions swirl in Cal's brain to the point of confusion. He just needs to let it all go and do what feels right in the moment.

"Cal, now that you've served your first couple of years on a Gen-One starship, and considering your resourceful-ness aboard the Etonic, have you given any consideration as to where you would like to serve next?"

"I have, sir, but it's all a bit of a jumble right now. I've been thinking about this for the last month. I'm not even sure what my options are to tell the truth."

"That's not surprising, Cal. You've been through a lot. I suspect you'll want to take a little time off, think it all through. That's fine. You should, Cal. You've earned it.

"Let me line out a couple of options. You can ask ques-tions, mull them over—make a decision in a couple of weeks if you need that long."

"Great. I'm looking forward to it, sir."

"So, Cal...Option one, I've discussed your exemplary service with the leadership board and we concur that you're to be promoted to Lt. First Class on the newest star-ship in the fleet, the USS Constellation. Not a commercial vessel, Cal, but a military heavy cruiser.

"This feels like a good fit for you. It is the most advanced starship to date. Hell, it practically flies itself..." the Doc pauses.

"But...?"

"But there is a second option. Leadership would like you to consider...I'd consider it a personal favor...We're in a bad way Cal...

"Option two involves another stint on a Gen-One. Now wait, before you comment, hear me out.

"As you know, the Etonic was sabotaged by two seasoned crew members. Now what I am about to tell you does not leave this table. Understood?"

"Yes sir. Of course."

"Good, good. We've been caught flat-footed, Cal. The Allegiance doesn't know when the next strike will come.

"Clearly, our counter intelligence is lacking, but that can be rectified. We need good men to try to crack this nut. If this...this resistance, for lack of a better word, had been successful in blowing up the Etonic...

"Er, sorry, Cal. You know what I mean. If our supply line and exports had been compromised, we would be at an extreme disadvantage. We may have assumed it was an unfortunate accident, never discovering the real threat.

"We now know that these terrorists will likely target other ships. They'll keep trying until they're successful. We have more than forty of these old Gen-Ones in service. They won't be decommissioned for the next eight years.

"We plan to have one or two covert crew members aboard each of the Gen-Ones, until new ships come online to replace them. Our focus is on the Gen-Ones, as they are particularly vulnerable to attack."

"And you want me to be a spy," Cal says flatly.

"Yes, we'd like you to consider another commission on a Gen-One, as an operative, Cal. You'd get double pay, a risk bonus, your own stateroom, and special perks. Secretly you'd still be a commissioned officer, but you'd have to blend in with the men, and watch for anything out of place, any suspicious behavior or activity. You'd be our first line of defense, Cal.

"I can't order you to do it, and I'd understand if you decide to board the USS Constellation instead. It might be what I'd do in your shoes. It might be what you *should* do. But, we're in a bad way, son, and you have the gumption and experience to pull this off.

"That's it, Cal. I'll leave it to you to mull over. Weigh it carefully."

"Thanks, sir. I will. I'll get back to you in a couple days, sir."

"Great. Whatever you decide will be the right decision."

Getting up from the table, the two shake hands and look each other in the eye. They nod, but say nothing more.

"Goodbye, Cal."

"Goodbye, Doc."

The two turn and part ways, walking in opposite directions. Cal pauses for a minute. A thought occurs. He turns toward the doctor, choosing his words carefully.

"Sir, I should do what you suggest, wait a couple weeks to make my decision. But I'm not going to do that. While I was serving on the Etonic, I watched a man die performing above and beyond his duty. He was a good man, he saved me and everyone on that ship. He knew he probably wouldn't make it, sir, but he did it anyway. That really made an impression on me.

"I also witnessed a dedicated team working tirelessly to keep the Etonic in top performance. The men work with little prospect of a different future. Yet, for their dedication they are kept in the dark about their mission, they have no view beyond the interior of the cabin, and worst of all...worst of all, they're not provided protection from the radiation emitting from the uranium ore.

"My father was a miner. You probably didn't know that, sir. He died from over exposure working the mines. So when I got on the Etonic and discovered the Allegiance doesn't protect it's own men from the very fuel that's necessary to fly? You can't possibly know what was going through my head.

"No wonder the Allegiance has internal enemies when it treats its own men this way. So that's the condition of my acceptance. Shielding for the men at the very least."

The Doctor pauses, taking time to reflect on how he might respond. He was going to remind Cal that being exposed to billions of high-energy particles emitted by the Van Allan belt during space flight is just as bad or worse. But he knows this is just an excuse. The men should be protected from internal and external radiation, all the same. When it comes to safety of ship and crew, cost cutting measures are indefensible.

"Cal, I can't make excuses for decisions made in the past. We've known about these problems for a long time. That's one reason the Gen-Ones are being phased out. But we can't do it overnight.

"Tell you what. There are forty Gen-Ones left. We'll be phasing them out, five over the next year alone. I can't promise you anything, but I'll bring this to the attention of high council. If I can't convince them, then I'll back channel extra shielding for a retro-fit on all the Gen-Ones. That's the best I can do, Cal."

"That feels like a start in the right direction."

"So, is that your answer, Cal? Will you sign on for another Gen-One mission?"

"Considering all of what you've said, I feel I owe it to Rusty, somehow. And I owe it to myself to find these people. And we *will* find them, sir.

"May I reserve a place on the U.S.S. Constellation after this next stint?"

"That's the spirit, Cal. I wish I had forty more like you. Yes, of course, of course. Consider it done. Give us a couple more years and the commission is yours. Do you have any other requests, Lieutenant?"

"Just one, Doc. I understand that Rodriguez Ortega has a commission on the Star Gull, I'd like to join him sir. We served on the Etonic together."

"I'm aware. The Star Gull is a fine ship Cal, and Rodriguez is a good man. Are either you or Rodriguez aware that the Star Gull has an all-women crew?"

"He neglected to mention that, Doc," Cal laughs, then ponders the idea in silence for a moment.

"Only two men on an all woman-starship? Could it be any worse than crewing with all men, sir?"

"I'm not going to speculate on that, Cal. But I will tell you it's a tight ship. Traditionally, it's all women, but times are changing. They are letting men serve, side-by-side.

"Is that what you want?"

"Do they sing songs on the Star Gull, Doc?"

"I imagine they do, Cal. I imagine they do."

"Then, yes. I'll take the commission."

"Excellent, Cal. Thank you. Good luck. I have a feeling you're going to need it."

"Well, sir, I guess that's about it. I need to pack and go through a briefing tomorrow at seven in the morning. Looks like I'm headed on another adventure."

"Yes, it certainly looks that way, Lieutenant."

Walking across the tarmac Cal turns toward his friend once more.

"Good-bye Doc.

"With clarity of spirit, through the darkness of fear, we will meet again in the twining light."

"And to you, young Lieutenant,

"I raise a glass to the fallen as we rise to meet our destiny in the stars."

ABOUT THE AUTHOR

Author D.K. Spencer likes his coffee strong and bold, the way he writes his science fiction. Bold characters. Strong ideas. That's why you're here.

D.K.'s story arc starts in a small Iowa town, roaming the ravines and back pastures behind his Grandma's house, searching for extraterrestrials.

Now he writes weird, humorous, dark, science fiction & fantasy short stories. Currently, D.K. is taking notes on alien life forms in an alternate universe. Or perhaps he's driving a blue '66 Ford pickup on back country roads with coffee in hand, looking for the lost land of dinosaurs. You just never know.

D.K. and his potter wife of twenty-six years, Gail, live with their companion cat in Portland, Oregon.

Songs of the Etonic is his debut YA novella.

Reach out. Stay informed. www.bignonioides.com

www.ingramcontent.com/pod-product-compliance
Lightning Source LLC
Chambersburg PA
CBHW070650130626
46555CB00006B/2796